The Shoshank Redemption

The Servant's Acknowledgments

I would like to thank Neil Wight, my editor and part-time servant to the Queen. I promise she'll be nicer to you, eventually. Koko misses you.

A sincere thank you to all of Shorty and Kodi's followers, especially those of you from day one.

To my kitties: growing up, I always knew I wanted to share my life with animals. What I didn't expect was the amount of love I'd receive in return. You guys are the best.

Finally, to Bryan, the other servant and amazing cat-dad: thanks for putting up with video equipment in the hallway, cameras covering the tables, computers and hard drives and books and calendars and questions and frustrations. But thanks mostly for being the one to suggest going to the shelter 9 years ago.

A Note About The Queen's Speech

In case it's not readily apparent, the Queen's voice is in quotation marks when she is audibly vocalizing in a trill or a hiss or a growl, and in italics when she is communicating silently through her expressions. If you've watched any of Shorty's videos, you know that her expressions, silent or otherwise, carry quite a lot of volume.

Table of Contents

In my stars I am above thee; but be not afraid of greatness! Some are born great, some achieve greatness, and some have greatness thrust upon 'em.

-William Shakespeare, *Twelfth Night*

Chapter 1

Sacrifice. No one knows the lengths I go to sacrifice all for them. Each could be slain through the night if 'twere not for my steady watch over the shadows; the almost imperceptible phantoms that frolic through the front room would surely bring death to us all if I didn't bat them away with an imperious *tap-tap*. Rowdy intruders threaten just outside the gate nightly but oh how my steely eye keeps them at bay. Not to mention that spiteful sprite perched halfway up the wall ready to attack at any moment. Oh how it mocks me, laughs at my attempts to smack it into oblivion as it remains, unmoved, night after night, taunting me. "It's just a spot," the Dimwits tell me repeatedly. But I know better, this cunning marauder that must be banished. I jump at it now, straining to scratch at the surface just beneath it, the revolting sprite just out of reach, and demand its surrender. "Out, damn'd spot! Out, I say!" I jump and I jump and I claw until I'm certain I've scared it into submission. A servant hollers, "Huzzah!" in appreciation from their sleeping quarters, and I am pleased.

Responsibility. I've not slept a wink this restless night while the Dimwits slumber, oblivious to the demons their mess has invited. Why have all my couches been moved? Why so much dithering hither and thither throughout the day? Battlements have been erected in disarray throughout the castle yet my cursed dainty limbs prevent me from ascending them for proper surveillance. The Simpleton is up there with nary a clue of what to do while I must protect the Dimwits from the floor. So many new corridors to investigate, enemy hidings to infiltrate. One might question me for not posting a trusted soldier to guard the castle rather than taking it upon myself. Find me such a worthy paladin within my keep and I'll find you a dog that doesn't reek of a hundred hairballs retched into a dirty litter box on a steaming hot day. Can't be done.

Empathy. Dull though they may be, my wards are endearing little chattels, earnest in their attempts to appease their Queen. They regularly offer gifts and a warm place to rest my weary head, heavy from the crown. Though I must be quite stern with them, they keep the dining schedule timely and are attentive to my poopsies. They even manage to scratch the hard-to-reach place just behind my ears that I can't quite access. Dainty limbs, you see. And indeed, 'tis amusing to hear them mumble inanities as they struggle with communication. I've managed to decipher a few idioms from their crude tongue, most notably "*treat-treats*" and "*fooood*" both spoken with an odd, rising pitch that is entirely annoying but nonetheless recognizable and ultimately rewarding. I've tried to teach them to use their ears and eyes instead of their mouths to communicate - should we venture out on a hunt together their foul sounds would surely give us away - but they stare at me like idiots staring into the sun and with as much comprehension.

Ah, my simple servants. They seek counsel constantly and I pity their dependence. They keep asking me who a good girl is, as if a Queen should have any information on the common townspeople below. They wonder aloud where their coins have gone when they could simply bend the knee and see how skillfully I've strewn them behind the couch which is also the treasury. They request the identity of the miscreant who vomits occasionally on the rug, as if a Queen would ever admit to such a transgression. But honestly who wove that thing anyway? Deserves to be vomited on if you ask me. Oh right, they did ask me. Well, it's neither here nor there. But if I had to do it, I'd do it there, not here.

But I sympathize with the disadvantaged so I disregard their musings. It's not their fault they were born limited in so many ways, nor is it mine should I feel the need to test their limits over and over and over again. All the better to understand them, you see. For example, I've determined that their vision is compromised at night, and stepping in front of them as they stumble to the water chamber mid-slumber is strictly for research purposes only. The fact that it also provides ample entertainment to me is simply good fortune. Thus, while their brains are grossly stunted, they are satisfactory in attending my needs and amusing to have around, so 'tis my duty to both protect and suffer the fools.

Leadership. To be a great leader, one must be diligent in keeping the forces ready to battle oncoming foes; I can't very well lead an attack with an unprepared army no matter how dense they may be. Perhaps it's time for a drill, that we may form our defense as a coordinated force. But then, something is telling me it's now too late. I sense the light of night beginning to change, a hum of hounds in the distance, a town rubbing the fog from its sleepy street eyes. Morning is imminent. I've been too easy on them. An attack is coming and the Dimwits are vulnerable. I can feel my pupils dilate, straining to see the perils before me. The dark is darkening and about to break. The flying rats outside could start chirping any second! Then where will we be? Vulnerable. Defenseless. We must make a stand post haste. Wait! Was that a chirp I just heard? Was it a beep? Do I know the difference? Yes! Surely it was! Either and or!

Cannon to the right of me! Cannon to the left of me! Cannon in front of me, volley'd and chirp'd! Ready or not, I must lead the troops into battle.

"Awaken, ye lot!" My rallying call pierces the silent, starless night. "A malevolent sun threatens to permeate these walls and diurnal creatures will surely arise and pull us asunder. Awaken, I say!"

No response. Nothing. The troops have failed me. Perhaps they are vanquished. Yes. 'Tis the only explanation for my abandonment. The Dimwits are dead. 'Tis I who have failed. I alone possessed the skill to protect the house, and though I stood steadfast in my duty, my army has fallen. An arrogant chirp echoes faintly in the distance. Could still be a beep. The township outside wakes and readies its forces without my permission nor preparation. I pace the corridor, defeated.

"O spiteful world, woe is *meeee*," I cry. "Why hast thou forsaken *MEEE? OOOHHH!*" Deserted by my people, I am left to fend for myself in these dark times.

I must check the rations, for who knows how long I have to endure this desolate existence. But what's this? My supplies are depleted. I've only enough food and water to last until my interest wanes which could be any second now. I continue down the corridor checking each chamber.

The castle is quiet, conquered. All lives lost. And yet, I remain. But for how long? Wait! What's this I see before me? An orb? A ghost! No, 'tis my Beautiful Tail! I pause to groom my Beautiful Tail and it feels comforting, calming, like a salve to the wound that is my despair. Oh, my Beautiful Tail, we have only each other now. Wait! This must be what they want, the approaching assailants. They want my Beautiful Tail! I groom it quicker, faster, with vigor, I've so little time to groom my Beautiful Tail! They can't get it. I won't allow it! I'll get it first! I twist around and around. My determination is as fierce as my tail is beautiful. I've got it! Now they can't have it. Ouch. What's that? A noise? Down the hall? In my head? The raid is upon us! Upon me! I shan't let the house fall. My battle cry is fierce and powerful as it thunders through the castle halls. "I am *QUEEEEN!* Here me *NOOOOWWWW!*" Oh, what's this I hear? A stirring. A whirring? A voice! Yes! A servant's voice! Oh, joyous day. I look to the left, I look to the right, and I pummel back down the corridor, buoyed by the evidence that my troops still live, to lead the onslaught against the impending morn. "This is my *HOUSE!* You shall not *PAAASSS!*" I screech the warning to the heavens and the dawn that threatens to invade any moment. The servants, apparently revived and well and inspired by my courage, have finally joined my chorus to defend these walls and stammer through a primitive vernacular in their most threatening way (which is quite comical if you ask me, but I keep encouraging them to try). We continue back and forth, my staff and I, until we are roaring in a frightening unison and I'm certain we have succeeded in defending the castle from all manner of invaders. "Well done, my people," I sing out. "We have bested a worthy adversary yet again. Let us celebrate in song!" Oh, excellent! A ward is doing one better and is joining me for a pre-morning exercise routine as we run about the grounds, drunk with victory. But they are heavy-footed and slack-limbed whilst I am nimble and quick and, oops, not so nimble I'm afraid, but the servants shouldn't have left that glass in the middle of the table directly in my path. I am the first to the end of the hall and back and around again, though they keep trying to catch up, all the while maintaining their "threatening" battle cry. Oh, my funny, feeble-minded folk, how you amuse me so.

The servant, pleased with assisting my courtly calisthenics, has provided provisions for my post-exercise feast and retired once again to their chambers. I shall wake them again with thanks and praise shortly, but first, a quick bite, and an assessment of the premises. The gate is secure. The walls are intact. No intruders detected. The Simpleton watches from on high like a half-baked black and white gargoyle. I nearly succeeded in forgetting its existence. I nose the air in the dope's direction. *Some help you were in the battle, you mashed-up Oreo rugrat!* I avoid direct eye contact lest it think me interested in, ugh, playing. But I know it's watching, so I squint my eyes and flatten my ears, more out of habit than an actual communiqué; the dolt can't decode which parts of its body are its own lest interpret observable language. I ignore its attention-seeking earflittings and head to the arrow-slits of the curtain wall.

Morning breaks. From my tower several stories high, I see the commoners below, the fluffy-tailed vermin skittering atop the town's dwellings, shiny and noisy elephants rumbling past, the obnoxious flying rats keeping their distance, and I am satisfied that all the day's creatures have fallen in line under my powerful gaze. Because I am a benevolent ruler, I announce to my house that all is well and serenade them with song, and their appreciation comes immediate and emphatic from the sleeping quarters, and it is good. My Queendom is prosperous and I look forward to extending my royal dominion but for now I shall lay on my back and allow a defeated, grateful sun to warm my full, fuzzy belly. Perhaps I can lull an errant hand there for a sacrifice later and it shall be amusing.

Chapter 2

I am awoken by a flurry of sound from a furrier mound. The Simpleton! It's wailing away about everything and nothing. *Get thee away!* I swat at the bothersome gnat to keep its distance. Seems it was spooked by some goings-on of the servants and misplaced itself next to me. *Yawn.* I adjust my head and roll onto my back to rest my weary soul just a bit longer; all this diligent castle-keeping has left me quite fatigued. Plus, the castle's concrete floor is hard on my feetsies. *A loft*, as our apartments are so named by the servants. Dimwits. I stretch and let a giant sigh flow through and lengthen my tired body and heavy limbs. Yes, so heavy. I can't move, my limbs feel so heavy. They're as concrete as this damned floor. My entire body, motionless. Queening is hard work, indeed.

...

I am awoken again by a commotion. Alas, I am not afforded the luxury to lie untroubled. For trouble is afoot! Or is it apaw? Having humans as one's only companions for so long has me quite confused. *Simpleton will you silence your wailing I'm trying to figure out if it's afoot or apaw!* I cast a quick stare of daggers at the nuisance that is currently wailing for attention. The servants are banging and clanging and barking and charging. Oh that I should enjoy a respite from the royal demands of not only caring for and protecting these servants but saving their very lives! Dimwits. They're erecting more walls and barriers throughout the grounds. *Must you make such a racket!* I turn my ears sidewise and downward. The servants may seem slow but they know exactly what I am saying. Expressing displeasure is an art form mastered by the feline, after all. *And I've plenty to express!* They are now pretending to ignore my protestations. *Yawn.* I shan't get a wink of deserved rest around here. I may as well investigate.

I shake off the sleep and lumber through a maze of barricades to a low wall being erected with what appear to be large green stones. Oh, how I love green! Hm. This green stone smells funny. I rub my cheek along its smooth, hard edge. Hm. Still smells funny. Like stale hope and old regret. Oh yes, cats can smell emotion. Hope smells like a ripe, freshly cut honeydew melon, a sweetness that is fragile and fleeting. But hope, much like a honeydew, turns rotten if held too long and becomes anger. I know because I once held hope the Simpleton was only visiting. Thus, anger smells of rotten fruit - apples, to be more precise - with acidic overtones and a crisp, caustic finish. One time a small apple somehow slipped beside and behind the ice box when I was pushing it there, and a fortnight later I couldn't tell if it was the fruit I was smelling or a servant's reaction at having again discovered a gift left for them in front of the litter box. Perhaps if they cleaned it more regularly, they'd smell less like rotten apples and the castle would smell less like my poopsies.

Regret, of which this strange green stone also reeks, resembles rancid milk that's just begun to curdle; at first you think you can tolerate it but a closer sniff causes a recoil in disgust, much like when I gaze upon the Simpleton. Contentment, my favourite scent, is like a plastic container or bag fresh from the market; I could chew on that all day. Sadness, oddly, is like a freshly opened can of salmon that you can't wait to slurp up and get rid of. The servants think me sympathetic when I attend to their sadness when all I really am is hungry.

Right now, all I can smell is a dried-up honeydew and rancid milk off this boulder, and, suddenly, a whiff of rotten apples wafts by. A servant's stump whips past and thrashes against my Beautiful Tail. I look up at the towering, disobedient servant. *Such insolence!* They are engaged in some harsh negotiation while the other one reinforces and stacks the green stones with urgency. I perceive no impending foe so I don't know what all the fuss of defense is for. I clean my Beautiful Tail fervently to rid it of the rotten apple scent left by my insubordinate underling. I'll steer clear of them for now until they smell better. I turn back to the green stone which stands just taller than I and twice my length, the width half as long, and set my front paws on the top edge to peek above its crest.

What's this? The rectangular stone is hollow, empty! It even slips a bit on the cursed concrete floor it's so slight. Some buttress this would be against a bombardment. Dimwits. I take several small inhalations from the cavity of the hollow stone to taste the rancid milk, the stale melon, and now a hint of lily - elation, excitement - and old sneakers which could be nostalgia or old sneakers.

Oh, wait! My poor wards were wrong, this isn't a war defense. 'Tis a box, a gift for their Queen! I leap happily into my new acquirement and roll about to lend my present a more pleasing scent. What rapturous sounds my claws make in this hard hollow shell. Scratching in this corner sounds like this: *scratch-scratch-scratch*. I wonder what it sounds like in that corner? I turn round in one swift motion to try and it sounds like this: *scratch-scratch-scratch*. Wondrous! I wonder if the result has changed in the previous corner? I flip over swiftly and try again. s*cratch-scratch-scratch*. Joyous event, it sounds anew! I wonder how deep my new hovel delves? I scratch at the floor, my claws sliding and scraping the surface in a symphony of sound. Try as I may, the floor doesn't give way, but dismayed I am not! *scratch-scratch-scratch*. A tornado of fur arises from my domain as I skillfully shuffle off my dead-ends and knots in a beauty regimen that is actually quite dignified though it may appear as if I am simply hurling myself violently side to side.

My spa day is interrupted by a thump against my green stone and I look up at the source. I see a hideous, blotchy patchwork of mayhem staring down upon me. The Simpleton! It dares try to invade my sanctuary? Oh how that face offends me. It's like a mad scientist was attempting to create an onyx feline beauty like myself when a raving white Labrador jumped in at the last second and out popped this one. It looks like a walking stuffed Rorschach test reject.

"HISS! I banish thee, ignorant encroacher!" It raises its muddy paw to swat but I am first with a deft left to the noggin. "HISS!

HA! You are no match for me, sullen Simpleton. Be gone!" It retreats and sulks away a few feet and pauses to look back. *Further!* scream my narrowed eyes, my ears sidewise.

This fort is mine. Enemies be warned. I peer just over the edge of my prize to spy any and all foes and remain absolutely still; ears, flattened; eyes, slits; stomach, grumbling. It's been at least several minutes since my last meal. Might that I waste away wouldst anyone care?

There is crashing all around me, explosions, defiances. An uprising? A mutiny! My forces have turned against me. Ingrates. No matter. I am protected within my magical green stone. I am a statue of strength and fortitude. I am invisible. I am invincible. No one can even touch me or, *BAHHH!* What's this? A strike on my Beautiful Tail! I twist around to see the Simpleton batting at my Beautiful Tail as she whips to and fro in a fury despite my wielding of power. My Beautiful Tail has a mind of her own, you see; I have no more control over her than I do the deceptive Simpleton. "Scat, you stunned skunk!" I let forth a barrage of insults as fatal as my blows. *tap-tap-tap.* It retreats yet I still see its feets on the precipice, a persistent paw with sheathed claws. "This is no time to play, you demented dalmation! We are under attack!" The Simpleton knows not the portent of the current events. This mutiny could surely result in the world's complete destruction, or at the very least a delayed nap! Then where would we be. I can't bring myself to imagine it.

The Simpleton seems to have understood and resigned its game, though it's more likely a servant drew near and it was afraid of being a "bad boy". It seems more keen on appeasing our servants than the other way around. Hasn't quite caught on yet how I've arranged the hierarchy in this land. Oh, here's an attendant now to attend to me. "I say, my good servant," I trill with a rising intonation of which they are so fond. "Have you come to offer me a gift? A treat-treat perhaps."

They're requesting information of me. No, they're suggesting I do something. No, they simply want to praise me. I nudge my nose in the air and trill again. "Yes, indeed, praise be to me, dutiful ward. That will be all." Their hulking hands descend quickly upon me and yank me from my sacred space. Perhaps something was lost in translation.

I am dumbfounded by the defiance. They've thrown me down to the ground in a helpless heap. Oh, what treatment I endure, the torture I must take. The giant's foot is within reach so I give it a punitive smack. *That will teach you!* I flit my right ear to advise against further breaches of conduct. They continue to bark at me while the other one begins placing objects into my green fort. I circle around the barking servant to investigate and jump back into my sanctuary. What's this? They're stocking my sanctuary with books, writing utensils, random wires, and their second-skins. "No, no, no, silly. I don't require any of these hindrances in my hideaway," I trill at the servant. "Remove all but the wires which I will enjoy chewing on. And the second-skins which I will enjoy lying on. In fact, throw them in the drying mechanism as I'll prefer them warm."

"Queen Shorty, no finer feline has ever graced this world nor ever will," the servant hails down to me. "You deserve all good things and more." Regardless of the accolades, I am once again yanked from my fort and hurled across the room like a child's plaything. Perhaps I mistranslated again.

So be it. This mindless mutiny can carry on without a Queen neither to overthrow nor throw around. Too much squawking and talking anyway. My third nap has been needlessly preempted by such buffoonery that I find myself quite flummoxed indeed. Calm now, Beautiful Tail. The longer you lash about the more likely you are to be stepped on by one of the slaves stumbling around. Dimwits. I spy the Simpleton staring at me from the servant's sleeping quarters. Seems it has had enough as well. *That's the best idea you've had all day*. I flit my left ear and saunter through to take refuge beneath the bed to wait out the storm. I lower my head below my shoulder line and maintain direct eye contact with the Simpleton while walking past. I let out a low grumble. "Sniff my butt and you're dead."

Chapter 3

A Lion's Lullaby

O'er the hem and 'neath the bed
I slink to rest my weary head
If something stirs and I should wake
The Simpleton's last breath I'll take.

'Tis just a little lullaby I wrote to repeat to myself to help calm the nerves and slip into sleep. I'd repeat it to the Simpleton if *it could tear its face away from its crotch for one second!* My silent scolding somehow interrupts its bathing and it looks up at me, both legs in the air, its head low, ready to dive back in. It looks like a splayed ampersand. *Yes, you, you crass cretin, I need my sleep so you best keep quiet!* It resumes the base ritual, seemingly unbothered, but my message was received. I curl in a circle and sigh with relief. I need my beauty sleep. I feel a whisp against my whiskers. Ah, yes, my Beautiful Tail also needs her beauty sleep! Yes, Beautiful Tail, *lick lick*, you may also rest and awaken with rejuvenated beauty, *lick lick*. I lift my legs to aid the cleaning process. I said it was crass, I didn't say it didn't get the job done.

...

I am roused by a loud racket just beyond the refuge of the bed. I know not what the servants are up to, though I'm certain it's no good, but I am way too comfortable to investigate. 'Tis safe and warm here under the cover of darkness. Especially warm. What's this? I feel a rising and falling of harsh quills against my back and crane my head to see a black and white lump lying next to me. I am warmed not by my surroundings but by the Simpleton itself! Seems it has curled up against my back, probably to irritate me, or perhaps out of fear of the chaos just beyond the bed's border.

Annoying. Yet warming. I allow the indiscretion as the heat pleases me and for once the Simpleton's not bounding about like a rabid fleabag. I nuzzle my nose back into my Beautiful Tail. *O'er the hem and 'neath the bed I slink to rest my ...*

...

Thunder. A storm rages. The attack comes from all sides. A million mice march toward me, each of them fuzzy and green with grey eyes and one yellow ear, the other having been torn off in a tantrum, a tattered tail in tow. They're angry, vengeful. No, not mice, much bigger than mice. Bananas. They've all turned into bananas! They grow larger as they draw closer. They smell not like catnip, like they usually do, but like apples. Rotten apples! Rotten, acidic, angry apples. I am besieged by angry, apple-scented bananas. I run and I run as they stampede toward me, but the floor is a cursed concrete and I can't make headway. The ground quakes, the castle shakes. The sky opens up. Literally. The sky is being carried away to reveal the merciless

29

heavens above as it becomes bright, so bright that it burns my Beautiful Tail.

What's this? I open my eyes as I am drenched in daylight as my protective mattress floats aloft. What phantoms are upon me that possess such skill? Oh, 'tis the minions maintaining their mess-making. They've carried the bed away. *I'm not done sleeping you insolent fools! Replace my cover at once!* They pretend not to understand my narrowed eyes but they know very well their crime. Punishment will be swift. *Simpleton, attack!* Where... where's it gone? The Simpleton's vanished. And after I allowed it to warm me mid-slumber. I shan't do that fool any more favors. A servant addresses me.

"My Queen, your beauty is as boundless as the sea, my love as deep. Might I petteth thee?" They reach down to touch me, but I am not placated.

"Human, how dare you touch me!" I hiss. "Here's two swats for a penance." I deliver two warning shots with swords sheathed. Should they try again they will taste my steel. They have retreated. The servants turn to each other to battle. Now's my chance to escape. I've not had a decent day's sleep, I'm not about to engage in a surprise cage match. I leap out of the bed-frame and run for cover, motionless for a moment as my claws can't gain traction on the blasted concrete floor.

I run down the corridor and round the corner. *Oof!* Too much speed on the turn and I slide into the wall. I gain purchase and proceed with haste. *Oof!* Where once was a passage is now a barricade. The maze I mastered not hours ago has been rearranged again. I lower myself close to the ground to avoid detection as I slither like a snake amongst the ruins of my house. Everything is different. Same smells, old smells, new smells, foreign smells. Oh, look, a green stone low enough that I may enter. I place my front paws on it and heave myself into it. *Oof!* It's solid! This one isn't hollow at all! The top is hard and flat. But it does offer a new vantage point. I think I can make it now to an even higher vantage, a nearby tower. I just have to extend a limb and, yes, I have it! I take hold of the tower's edge with my front legs. My back legs begin to slide on the slippery green stone. I've no choice. I must leap forward, short limbs or not. Faith of feline will carry me to safety. I jump. And I fall. But my front legs hold fast, my swords buried deep within the tower's edge formed from a porous material much different to the hard green stone. I claw and clamber my way up the vertical face to the summit. Success! I am a diligent climber and worthy victor. I see all, I know all. My Beautiful Tail cuts huge swaths through the air for all my Queendom to witness. I sit now and take stock of what has become of my land.

Interesting. Towers, barricades, battlements erected throughout. This will be most advantageous in defending the castle, especially since the servants provided a suitable means of ascent for their Queen. Perhaps I've been too harsh and misjudged them. My Beautiful Tail swishes in disagreement. Ah, you're right, Beautiful Tail, if I weren't stern with the servants they wouldn't have a clue how to care for their Queen and would surely perish. Oh, what's this? On my tower's corner lies an armament. A tool? A token! 'Tis a round green thing, a hollow circle, could fit round the Simpleton's head. *tap-tap.* It's a light oddity. *tap-tap.* Oh! Part of it is sticky! *tap-tap-tap.* I wonder what would happen if I sent it o'er the tower's edge? *tap-tap-tap*. And away it goes! Oh, a merry sound as it clunks against the concrete. Look how it rolls beneath the couch. Ah, 'tis good to be Queen. Go ahead, Beautiful Tail, swish away now unencumbered.

Oh, a ward approaches! "Good day, dutiful ward." I nose the air with a slight trill. The human offers a high-pitched salutation and a hand approaches cautiously. There are a myriad of scents coming off the hand but mostly cinnamon, odd since this one normally smells of peaches denoting a pleasant, cheerful disposition. Poor thing is stressed. I'm sure they need a pet which always calms them down and has them smelling more agreeable. I allow their fingers to scratch beneath my chin and beside my ear. One, two… *Ok, that's enough.* I pull my head away and stare at the hand, daring it to try again. I mustn't seem too easy on the servants, you see, lest they forget who's in charge. The servant congratulates me on being a fair Queen and leaves me once again to rule on high. They appear to be looking for something.

Oh! What's this I hear? A skirmish. A strike? A knock! At the gate! Tally ho, my troops! I shall gallop and greet the enemy. Make

33

way! I pummel to the floor in an admittedly inglorious heap - dainty limbs, you see - and tear down the corridor, ultimately reaching top speed. What's this? I stop running, sliding on the cursed concrete into a pile of overcoats. They've lowered the drawbridge without my consent. Fools! Now we'll all be slain this very... Oh, 'tis just one of my wards. *Well, how on earth did you lose your way such that you could not reenter?* I widen my eyes and turn my left ear quickly. The ward saunters by passing loose fingers across my brow. I stare at the drawbridge, again closed. The mechanisms and machinery beyond remain a mystery to me. On occasion I've set foot across the moat into the vast emptiness of space. Honestly, it was quite dreary indeed. Too many smells, too many sights, with not enough dens and too much daylight. No, I didn't like it a bit, no, not at all.

Dissatisfied with the soldiers, I saunter on to guard the drawbridge which also provides a good sightline down the corridor to view the goings-on. Well, it did provide a good sightline until the servants sullied this place. Shame. What once was a clean, unfettered foyer to the castle is now a rampant wreck of ruin. A shambles. Supplies are strewn throughout making it impossible to relax. No, this is no place for a Queen. I begin to withdraw back down the corridor when I get a whiff of fresh chilli pepper. Panic.

I venture through the rubble of the foyer to the side room and the source of the scent. And there, sandwiched between a tower of green stones and a pile of rectangular pieces that once hung on the wall lay a small container, enclosed except for thread bars criss-crossed all around. Through the threads I see a ghastly, blemished nose and eyes, diverted and hypnotized, staring at something, yet nothing. The Simpleton. One of its lazy eyes looks like it's trying to escape the cage. *Well, how did you get trapped in there, Simpleton?* My ears aflutter with the quick transmission. The Simpleton is silent. It stares blankly, solemnly. I approach the cell for closer examination. *Aye, ye silly sod, you've allowed yourself to get captured and I suppose you expect a pardon, yes?* I press my nose against the bars and inhale the pepper of panic. The Simpleton's nose butts up ruthlessly against my own. "HISS! How dare you touch your Queen!" I raise a swift paw and bat at the cage. "From hell's heart I stab at thrrrlll?" I trill unconsciously as I'm suddenly hoisted aloft. What's this? A surprise attack! I am overthrown. "I am QUEEEN!" I shriek. "Put me DEOOOWWWN!" The sky thunders with my demands as I twist and coil but the giant's hands are powerful, inescapable. I am bandied about like a child's hand-me-down toy, jolted and jerked, this way and that. "Who dares handle me? Release me, barbarian, so that I may scratch your eyes out!" The buffoon heeds my demand and hurls me, carelessly, into a tiny, dank dungeon. Before I can even raise a paw to strike I hear a *zzziiippp* as darkness envelops me. I turn round as best I can in my cramped quarters that I may gaze upon my ruthless aggressor. And I stare into their eyes with disbelief. The servant. MY servant! Deceived by the very hand I let pass my ear unscathed not minutes ago. Oh, but betrayal tastes bitter much like *the blood that you will surely shed upon my escape!* My eyes, mere slits, my ears flattened to the side as I ready to pounce on the perpetrator. The servant stands, only their foul feet within my sight, and I let out a low, lingering growl.

"You're lucky I'm in here slave, lest you lose an achilles with one swift swipe!"

Frightened, the slave retreats. I am left alone in the dungeon. But I am not undone. I paw my surroundings, an odd prison of cloth woven with a coarse thread and a mesh tapestry. The walls have some give yet seem impermeable to my swords. It smells faintly of pepper and catnip and vinegar. The scent triggers the visual of a White Giant with prodding hands and torturous interrogation devices. I now recall the last time I was quarantined in this confinement. I had forgotten the treachery of the humans, the laughter as I was persecuted, crucified for being a complacent Queen. 'Twas I who laughed last, licking the blood of the White Giant off my cunning claws.

I now know why the Simpleton was panicking. It would appear the mutiny is complete. The humans have bested the best and I've no idea how or why. They hurry to and fro, grunting, arguing, their hooves heavier than normal as they stomp past my prison. I hear the drawbridge open and close several times, the echoes of banging and clanging growing ever louder within the castle. And more voices ringing, more clogs trampling through, a river of commotion flowing by at a furious, turbulent pace, the ashes of ruin raining down as pirates storm the castle to plunder what remains. Alas, I am beaten, powerless. There are no stands left to make, no hideaways to investigate, not even a tiny treat-treat to be had. Beneath me lies a second-skin of a servant, green, with the scent of calming chamomile and plastic bags filling my sorry cell. But I am neither calm, nor content. I can't stand to see anymore so I turn away from the world in my tiny hovel to face complete darkness and plan my counter-attack when I escape. Oh, what a whirlwind of terror I'll unleash on my tormentors!

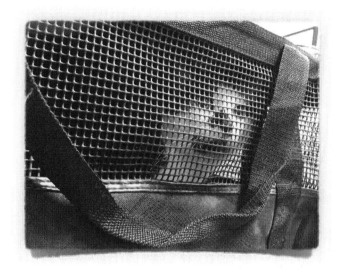

Chapter 4

After several attempts at escape, I believe I've found a weakness in my domain. The prison's hem is a woven cross-stitch, a tough twine that feels flimsy yet firm. From what I can discern, the front, back, one side, and top of my cell are all adorned in a mesh through which to see. I've tried slicing my way through the front and side but this drew too much attention from the servants who arrived quickly to thwart my getaway.

But at the top corner I spot a sliver of light seeping through. I've pawed gently at the space and am certain I've expanded it. There is also a pleasing sound that results. *clink-clink.* I see something moving just beyond the space, a small thing bouncing up and down in response to my batting. *clink-clink.* What could it be? A flea? Too big to be a flea. A mouse? Too small to be a mouse, and my frame of reference informs me that all mice are green and fuzzy with one misshapen yellow ear. 'Tis a new infiltrator, I suspect, one that warrants further study. *tap-tap-tap. clink-clink-clink. bat-bat-bat. clink-clink-clink.*

Well, this is getting me nowhere. The miniature mouse refuses to fear me and has lost my interest. But, wait. The sliver of light is no longer a sliver but has since grown to a full beam! I bet I could pass a paw through. I sit up tall on my haunches and gently reach through the opening with my front left leg. It fits! I extend my claws to grasp the exterior wall. Now what? Surely I can't fit through that small opening. Not that I'm portly, mind you. Generously proportioned, some might say. Rightly rotund? For your edification, the excess flesh on my abdomen is actually called a primordial pouch, an extra bit of skin round the belly whose purpose has confused humans for eons. Their theories range from protecting the abdomen during battle, ease of extension when running, or simply expanding to fill our gullet.

None of this is true. No, it's just where we store extra hairballs for convenient and voluntary expression of displeasure. You thought it spontaneous? Heavens, we felines always have the time to make it to the unsightly rug or to a servant's shoe before doing the deed. Planned, dear reader, all a plan.

Speaking of which, my current plan needs some work. My limb poking through the canopy has squashed all but a freckle of light seeping through. Oh, but my luxurious fur surely takes up some of the space, half at least! I push my nose along my outstretched leg to the opening. Ah, I am powerful indeed as the passage opens further, wider. My head is free! Now above the canopy, my eyes quickly scan my surroundings.

Detritus everywhere. No clear path of departure. Voices in the distance. Booming footsteps echo through the castle. Voices getting nearer. Footsteps drawing closer. I've no time to route my escape. I must act now. I struggle to pull myself up with my left leg, still latched onto the outside of this contraption, but my hind legs aren't long enough to lurch me onward, my forward right leg clawing aimlessly within my prison. I jump and jump with no progress, but I hear a clinking sound. Just to my left I see my little ally that aided my escape which was not a mouse after all. 'Tis just a bauble. A trinket! *Til we meet again, tiny friend. I bid thee farewell!* I become a cyclone of madness in my final push to freedom.

"My Queen!" A voice exclaims from above.

Damn! The insurgents are upon me. I've been foiled. I fall back into my enclosure pulling my head through the opening. But my front left leg is stuck outside the enclosure. Trapped. The rebels have somehow clamped my left paw to the exterior when I was clawing it. I pull and I yank and hiss at my confines. "Release me, foul cell!" A servant's hand comes into view, surely to cast the final blow in the insurrection. They grab onto my fastened foot. "How dare you trap me, traitor! I cast thee out!" A swipe with my right and a roaring hiss have frightened the brute away, but only after I successfully freed myself from the shackle. Flattened on the dungeon floor I see the beam of light shrink to a sliver and then disappear altogether, a *zzziiippp* punctuated with an exclamatory *clink!*

Captured yet again, I resign myself to the darkest corner of my confinement. If death should come, tell it I'm busy napping.

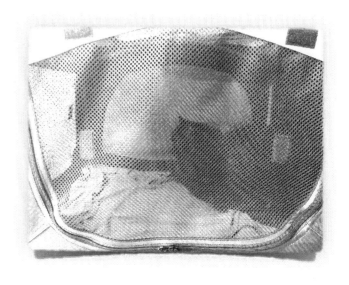

Chapter 5

Movement. An earthquake? A twister! Yes, I've flown aloft, my cell and all! Everything is a blur as I'm jostled side to side, hurled to and fro. Perhaps I'll be fortuitous and land on someone wicked; the perpetrator who entrapped me, for instance. I manage to turn round to get a better view through the mesh, my legs scrambling beneath me to find balance. I get caught up in the servant's lovely green second-skin and suddenly feel all warm and fuzzy because of it. Dammit! No, I am angry, enraged, quite affronted indeed! Oh, but the second-skin does smell fine. But, oh, how I am besmirched!

Wait! What's this? We're leaving castle. I've not been beyond the moat since I can barely remember. Not since… no, it can't be.

We are destined for the White Giant! No, no, this is not good, not good at all. "Turn round this instant!" I cry out with all my royal might. "I'll tear you and this vile cell and that White Giant to shreds!" The world flies by my cage at too quick a pace. I am inundated with too many smells, too many sights, too many sounds. I want to bury myself in the dark corner but I must stay vigilant, watching for any ambush, daggers at the ready.

We're descending into a valley as strange fowl squawk and chirp and chime forebodingly. *Thud.* My cell and I have been flung to the floor which reeks of wet canine and urine, and also a mild citrus detergent that was meant to block both. *Blech.* I hear the rising squeals of my disloyal drudge. They have bent the knee and are peering one eye into my cage, just beyond a claw's reach unfortunately. "You are captured, Queen. We are taking you to the White Giant. Your reign has ended."

"And yet I remain," The ground trembles as I let out a drawn-out rumble. "You will pay for this treachery. And by the by, your lovely green second-skin comforts me only a little!"

Oof. Hoisted aloft again, I'm hurled backward, now covered completely with the second-skin. I shuffle it off just enough to free my face and now wear it as a cloak. Such indignity. Oh, but look how it shrouds everything but my eyes. A disguise! I am invisible. I see the world but the world sees me not. A door opens. Commotions. A field of servant stumps stomping past. I hear a clicking noise, a clacking, a thwapping, servant voices old and new, a panting. A snout! Before, me, a lout, slurping and burping! Despite my disguise it has sniffed me out! "How dare thee, dog! Shoo, you vile vermin!" I hiss and holler, and I attempt to smack its nasty nose into oblivion but I catch the second-skin and it goes over my head. Covered again, my humiliation complete, I try to save face by letting out one more tumultuous roar but even that ends in a comical cackle, befuddled as I am.

So that's it then. Servant and swine have conspired against me. I hear the mutt's muted sniffings and wheezings, more voices, and feel the jostling of motion once again.

I would take stock of my surroundings but am blinded by green. I take comfort in not seeing anyway. My defeat is complete. I don't even protest or flee when I'm dropped to the ground and hear the *zzziiippp* and *clink* and the high-pitched address. The servant removes my cloak. I deny them the satisfaction of my pleas but hurl daggers with my eyes nonetheless. Again my prison is shuttered and we set off. Now we are beyond the land's border crossing fields into the fray. I feel a rising as the servant heaves me higher but then my view is cut off; methinks the front of my cell is now held against the servant's chest, their arms enveloped around the prison. I could claw out their very heart if I had my druthers! Alas, all my options lie scattered at my feet like shed claw sheaths and fur balls. But the lack of visual stimulation is somewhat calming, my surroundings somehow familiar. I take a deep breath, what feels like my first in a very long time, and sigh with a great deal of resignation and perhaps, even, the slightest bit of relief.

Nope, just resignation.

Chapter 6

A month has passed without nourishment. Perhaps a year. A fortnight surely. Honestly, the precise observance of time has never been an interest of mine; a Queen never acknowledges its passage except when it pertains to feedings, nappies, and the malodorous moments passed after poopsies. Thus, I've chosen simply to ignore the concept altogether. But I am certain I've languished in solitary for at least forever.

Thud. My cell is dropped down discourteously. What's this I see before me through the mesh barrier? The Simpleton! It faces me from its own crude cell, much smaller than mine. Indeed my prison could hold twice as many, thrice! Aye, it surely befits a Queen compared to the sullen Simpleton's confines. *'Tis a palace these fine mesh walls compared to your sorry surroundings!* I convey to the daft dolt. *Stop staring at me and flitting your ears, I don't know our destination either.* Surely its mother gave birth in a tree and this one fell from the tallest branch.

Bang! The earth just shook as if the universe had suddenly been snuffed out, the sun extinguished. I nearly lost a life from fright alone! I am drenched in near-darkness. What plague has now befallen me? I've been pitched in a pit, buried alive, like some cast-off good-for-nothing runt of a litter. *No offense, Simpleton.* One of its lazy eyes literally looks like it's about to take leave of its host.

The sun, at least, has ceased its vexation, all outside commotions muffled. I'm in some sort of room. A tomb! Left to lie and die with no company but my own. *Silence, Simpleton, let me think!* 'Tis under the shield of darkness when I am truly powerful, omniscient. The blackness of dark matches my coat and I let my eyes pierce the night to hunt for an egress, the servants nowhere near to thwart my escape attempt this time.

Through the cross-stitch windows I can see my enclosure appears entirely blocked. I paw again at my surroundings. To my right, the sturdy textile wall is malleable but as yet impassable. I paw again and again and again, scraping my swords against the strange material. I can't give up, I won't! *scrape-scratch-scritch-scratch*. Hm. There is no change. Or perhaps there is. *scratch-scritch-scrape-scratch*. Quite a pleasing sound, really. Let's try with the other paw, my right, which isn't as deft as my left, but let's give it a go. *scrape-scrap-scritch-scratch*. It's proving quite hypnotic, rhythmic, sonic. *scrape-scratch-scrap-scritch*. As my muscles move, my mind stills, my focus hones. The repetition is calming, familiar. I forget now where I am, even what I am doing. I am scraping this strange textured wall for some reason again and again and nothing is changing, yet still I persist. But everything is changing. I am not trapped simply because another tells me it's so, for my mind flows freely into and through and out these walls. Indeed, I've never felt so free here in my protected sanctum. *scratch-scrape-scritch-scrape*. That enlightenment should arrive in shadows ebony as my fur delights me not a little. *Witness it, Simpleton! Witness the grandeur of my ascension!*

If I weren't busy being enlightened, I might have noticed a *click*. And a *creak*. And the blasted light of day suddenly shining down upon me. But I am lost in my meditation. *scratch-scrape-scrawl-score*. Score! I've made a mark! Produced a puncture! Alas, my sword is stuck! I pull and yank at the textile wall, now seemingly made of stone, and I'm suddenly aware of the sunlight and the shrill yapping of my servant's voice. "Oh, my Queen, trying to escape the boot of the carriage are you? Pointless!" And suddenly I am ascending alright, just not in the transcendental sense. My cell and I have again been lifted up, jogging me side to side which has freed my sword from the stone.

The view from my prison passes fast but I'm sure I just caught a glimpse of hellhounds near by, their offensive snouts sniffing me out to bring about my demise. Come closer, ogres, and I shall slice thy snouts and throats! Another *thud*, a *slam*, a *chug*. I believe my chamber and I have been placed on the servant's lap, the warmth familiar even through the coarse fabric beneath. A container has been set next to mine. *Oh, Simpleton, you're here again! I keep forgetting on purpose that you exist.* It stares at me blankly from its cage that has been placed facing mine. The ground below me trembles and grumbles. My brow furrows and my ears slant back as I let out a grumble of my own. "I say, slave, I find the manner of my transport most disagreeable." The slaves don't bother to notice my annoyance of the turbulence of their carriage. I look to the Simpleton for a hint of assistance, a sign of situational awareness, a single note of intelligence, and find not a one.

I must admit the Simpleton is my greatest failure as Queen. He arrived to my Queendom a forlorn, fussy little shrimp of a thing, with boldness and flair and not a brain cell to spare. He stood up to the servants which amused me, and he stood up to me which intrigued me. The nerve it would take to challenge all within the castle, a pint-sized speck no bigger than the tip of my Beautiful Tail, I thought him destined a knight or a ninny, but I wagered on the former.

At first, he was so brash he was boorish, climbing the servant's legs like trees, going potty in the planters, clawing the furniture like a feral beast, and I disciplined him upon every misconduct. After a week of corrective action, he fell in line and I accepted him as my apprentice; the fact that I needed to expand my army to adequately defend the castle certainly had much to do with my decision.

Though he was initially disobedient, the one trait that was immediately redeemable was his watchful eye, lazy as it was. (Because it certainly wasn't his appearance. My heavens, he was unpleasant to look at. Ears too big, eyes wide-set, and he looked permanently filthy, like an albino rabbit that fell into a puddle of black ink.) He followed me everywhere, did everything I did, ate where I ate, scratched where I scratched, slept where I slept. He even proved a fair sword-fighter and himself a nimble competitor in our military drills, sprinting the lengths of the castle's corridors back and forth and back again. We laid out surprise attacks on each other several times a day keeping our skills and our minds sharp. Though he never quite understood the point of my morning and evening rounds - checking the entire castle for intruders, weaknesses, shadows, and sprites - he nonetheless proved an earnest pupil and, dare I say it, a trusted comrade.

But, over time, he insisted on doing the one thing I did not give him permission to do.

He grew. Tall. His legs soon became so long he could jump to the counters and the tables, climb ladders with ease, and even leap tall iceboxes in a single bound. The dirty rascal would climb the castle and act like a king. I swear he'd be laughing at me from his new heights, my petite frame preventing me from following suit. And he soon took advantage of his stature. If I were hunting the green fuzzy mice, he would get overly excited and leapfrog over me and bound off the walls and take the prize for himself. There was no thrill of the kill to be had for the Queen! Even whilst I slept, he would rouse me with a surprise attack, not understanding there was a time and place for such things. It became ever so tiring fighting off a lanky lout who couldn't control his increasing strength. But all of it I could forgive, every transgression I could forget, if he had just stopped being so damned dependent.

For example, if I was getting pet-pets from the servants, he would get so jealous he'd leap up and challenge me for a place on their lap. Wherever the servant would go, especially the one who smells like peaches, the Simpleton would follow. No longer was he loyal to the

Queen, he soon favored the slaves! The second they would leave the castle he would start wailing away as if abandoned by his mother. Upon their return, he would wail away asking why he was abandoned. It was embarrassing, really. He stopped standing up to them, and never did he ever commit even the most comical misconduct against the humans, so afraid he was of being called a "bad boy." Some soldier he turned out to be. If there's one thing I absolutely won't tolerate, aside from dirty litter boxes, more than two belly rubs, the roaring rug menace, shadows, small sprites perched halfway up walls masking as spots, half-empty food bowls, strangers, cages, and rotten apples, it's simpletons. Thus, through a lot of aggravation, my once-trusted apprentice became little more than a nuisance to me and I soon regarded him - it - as nothing more than a jester in my court. And now, with the ground beneath us trembling, heading to parts unknown and a fate uncertain, it stares at me from behind its bars in absolute panic. The helpless Simpleton could have been so much more if it stayed in line under my capable paw. Surely death would come swift if forced to fend for itself. Now I look upon the dunce with such disappointment, a tiny bit of loathing, and not a little resentment. The current ordeal seems to have struck the Simpleton dumb, muted by fear and panic. I flick my right ear sideways and back, leering at the traitor. *If we were in the same cage, I'd give you something to panic about.*

I was unprepared for the sudden lurch and I'm thrown to my side mid-leer. "My Queen," a slave addresses. "We hath arrived at the destination of your doom. Prepare for the fury." Movement. My cell and I are being transported again, *and with very little care!* I'm tossed tumultuously about while they avoid addressing my displeasure. Dimwits.

More servants on their stumps plodding past, the scent of stale and fresh dog urine all around, chirps and beeps and honks and bells pierce the putrid air, my prison paraded through the streets of town. My Beautiful Tail strains to swish as she is caught beneath the second-skin. 'Tis an inglorious end to my reign, this march, but at least I look good in green.

We exit the town through a series of glass gates and enter what I assume to be the torture chamber of my undoing. The White Giant, with their cold instruments and prodding fingers, will be no match for the wrath I will wreak upon my release!

But something seems awry. There is always a scent dissonance within the White Giant's quarters, an uncomfortable juxtaposition of fear, recently disinfected floors trying to mask excrement and wet-dog, and treat-treats. Absent even are the fetid odours of the sanctimonious White Giants themselves, a sickly blend of citrus and vinegar. No, this is a different station of suffering entirely. This fortress reeks of strong chemicals and I have the sudden urge to urinate everywhere. The floor is adorned in rugs that smell artificial but are not altogether repugnant, lined with a light fur with a perfect pattern of black patches. Somehow I believe it to resemble the coat of a leopard though I've never seen one in the wild. Well, I've never been in the wild, so what would I know? Putrid place it would be, existing among the commoners of the wide open. I've heard tell that you don't get treat-treats whenever you desire them. I can't even begin to think about how to imagine what it could possibly be like.

A silver gate slides opens and we enter a small room that smells of wood and metal and corrugated cardboard and slave sweat. The servant speaks to me in a rising intonation that doesn't imply impending doom at all but I'm not so easily swayed. The gate opens again and I am escorted down a long corridor with the same rug I saw and smelled before, a scent that could only be improved with a squat here and there, and over there, and over there.

I've been placed on the floor, gently this time. *Oh, what magnanimity, slaves!* Dimwits. That I might forgive such transgressions past through meagre niceties. Methinks not! There appears to be a solid gate before me. Nay, a drawbridge.

A *click.* A *chunk.* The drawbridge is opened. I am carried in and, again, set down lightly on the floor, its surface a bleached wood that is not at all like the cold, foul-smelling ground I was expecting. If the White Giant changed quarters since the last torturing this is at least an upgrade.

The Simpleton is next to me, surely having quite the fit having lasted this long without its beloved servant fawning over it like a feeble baby. But what's this? The servant bends the knee and addresses the Simpleton like, well, a feeble baby! I hear the now familiar *zzziiippp* and watch as it escapes its enclave, none the worse for wear, but honestly who could tell with that mottled mug. The servant picks it up and leads it away and I am thankful. At least I can lie alone with my thoughts, peaceful that the journey has, for the time being, ended. Perhaps the White Giant has already begun the persecution and I am next on the chopping block. Or perhaps the Simpleton is free! I hear it wailing away now, the Dimwits speaking in their piercing pitches. Why doth I remain entrapped whilst morons run amok? They've all conspired against me, surely. The jester, it seems, plans to have the last laugh whilst I meet my doom trapped in this dungeon. But I shan't. I won't! I am still Queen, after all. I shall rule with an iron paw until my last dying breath! Or at least until my next nap, whichever comes first.

A servant kneels down next to my cage, the one who is often more tranquil and smells of buttered toast, and addresses me softly. "Oh, my

Queen, art thou prepared to meet thine end?"
zzziiippp.

I see a space reveal itself at the front of my cell just as I am willing it open. Yes! My gaze is powerful indeed as I have managed to unravel the tapestry of my prison. Now is my chance to escape. I peek my head out, the White Giant nowhere in sight. I take a cautious step, and another, and another, keeping close to the floor, wary of all threats in this new territory. Freedom feels good, as does the wood floor which feels soft on my feetsies, but I mustn't let my guard down for the White Giant and their army could strike at any moment. I look to the left and to the right. It appears I am in a vestibule off a corridor, not dissimilar to my castle in fact. I turn to the left, gliding across the floor surreptitiously, being so covert that none can see that I've freed myself from the dungeon. The servants continue their shrill speak acting as if everything is normal, but they are dullards and can't see me as I glide so close to the floor, stealthy as a ninja. I come upon a small room, a closet. What's this? A poopsies depository. My poopsies depository! Smells just like home. What manner of puzzlement is this predicament? Where is the White Giant? Where is the onslaught? Where is the army of my destruction? I slink around a corner, careful not to be bludgeoned to death by unknown interlopers. I enter a small room to my left filled with green stones stacked to the ceiling. I make a note of the opportune hiding spots between and behind them. I continue down the corridor, servants following for some reason since I am not visible when camouflaged as a ninja, the Simpleton wailing, familiar smells of castles past floating by. More green stones, cardboard boxes, and a rug. My rug! Yes, 'tis my rug! I sniff it disbelievingly. Even now I can smell the vomit of displeasure I will express upon it in due course. And there's my couch, my chair, my glass table I lie on when I need a servant's attention, and my side table that must be cleared of all objects all of the time, especially when I need a servant's attention. 'Tis the remnants of my castle strewn about this new place! Aye, the servants rescued all of my possessions after the previous onslaught and secured a new castle for my ruling. A curious benefaction considering they have led me to slaughter.

"Queen! My Queen!" a servant hollers, kneeling down in front of me. I stop in my tracks, widen my dilated eyes and turn my ears sideways. *You can see me? Are you a wizard?* I approach their outstretched fingers cautiously and take several shallow sniffs. Cardboard, plastic bags, peaches, memories of cinnamon. This servant is currently content and pleasant. Perhaps they've gone mad. I look around quickly and back at them. *Where hast thou taken me? Can't you see? This castle is different, disorderly, defenseless. Man the catapult human, trouble is apaw!*

"Queen, my benevolent Queen, thou hast successfully procured through royal demand the acquisition of a finer castle and henceforth we seek only to serve thee until Queendom come."

Well, I indicate by nosing the air, *that will be all then.*

They reach a hand out to touch my crown but I back away and raise a paw. *You imprisoned me for an eternity and I shan't forgive so easily, human!* Frightened, the servant retreats and scurries away.

I take refuge behind a tower of green stones, still uncertain of the servants' objectives, and become invisible while keeping one eye trained on them. (I am only visible to the servants if they can see both my eyes; I'm not sure why, it's just how it works.) Thus, with just one eye glaring at the mouth-breathers, I can see they have retired to the couch and are dining on something that smells disgusting, though the box it came in looks enticing. They're eating, talking, laughing, looking around the castle, pointing, plotting, conspiring. After I freed myself from prison, they haven't seemed intent on throwing me back in or reprimanding me. Must be some ploy to gain my trust. Oh, what a tangled web they must be weaving to overtake the throne. I feel my brow furrow, my ears turning back against their foul guffaws, my Beautiful Tail cutting huge low arcs which they can not see. I watch them with one squinted eye as they now move about the castle planning my demise and I vow to rage, rage against their insurrection for I shall not go gentle into that good -

"Shorty, *foooood?*"

My eyes widen and my ears turn forward. *Oh heavens, that does sound pleasing.* I saunter over with a tall, curved Beautiful Tail to the servant who has prepared a kill for me. "Prepared a kill for me, have you, ward?" I trill.

"Queen Shoshobeans, might that I appease my Queen with a bounty of mice entrails and duck confit?"

"I say, that will do nicely," I trill again and nose the air. The dutiful, repentant slave has acknowledged the error of their ways and is preparing my feast on the counter. A *crack*, a *creeeaaak*, a *slurp*, and the *clinking* of metal on glass as they skin and bone and braise the prey. They set my meal before me on the floor. I sally up to sniff the kill, but then I recall the ordeal of the day and glare up at the remorseful rebel, my Beautiful Tail swishing this way and that does all the talking. *I am pleased with the provisions but not at all with you. Get thee away!*

The servant has done as I asked and let their Queen be but I watch them as they retreat to ensure no infringement on my dining. The Simpleton sidled up to my bowl when I wasn't watching and is helping itself to my meal, the servants having provided just one offering this eve. Perhaps supplies are scant, or there are few beasts roaming this part of the land that we must ration our fare. I walk up beside the Simpleton and place my head on top of its head and apply pressure, my front leg wrapping round to straddle its neck. *Oh, no, Simpleton, this won't do at all. You know the rules. The Queen eats first and the Jester has what is left. Go Jest somewhere else until I'm finished.* The Simpleton obeys and skulks away. Miraculously, it has shut up but keeps lurking around as if it lost its soother, continually looking to the servants for allowance to explore the new surroundings. *You are a disappointment and a disgrace to the Queendom, you harried Holstein cow!* It ignores my umbrage, or doesn't understand. Probably the latter. At peace, I can finally enjoy the hunt of the day.

A few minutes - perhaps it's hours? - later I hear the distinct sound of crinkling plastic from a chamber down the corridor. I lick my chops and proceed to the room where the servants appear to be assembling my bed frame. *Ah, it is good*, my Beautiful Tail announces with a curvaceous whip of the tip as I meander to the middle of the room to take a seat for proper supervision. I lick my paw to wash my face and am interrupted by a servant's voice which is louder than usual. "My Queen, thou art more

beautiful than all the Queens in all the lands!"
Methinks they are trying on their threatening
tone, but that doesn't accord with their praise.

*Silence, servant, your voice vexes me not a
little*, my Beautiful Tail a whip, my paw raised
mid-wash.

"Queen Shoshobeans, you have a
Beautiful Tail! SO BEAUTIFUL!"

*Slave, I am aware, now cut your tone by
half or I'll halve your tongue.* Indeed, the
origins of the phrase, "cat got your tongue" is
because we simply refuse to tolerate shouting,
and humans are too loud most of the time.

The slave knows well not to approach
their Queen but responds insolently by hurling a
tomato at me. Can you imagine, the insolence!
Oh, what's this? It's not a tomato, it's some sort
of vermin, a roundish rodent, a white weasel of
a thing. I paw at it and it makes a glorious
scratching sound along the wooden floor. Oh,
look at how it seeks to escape by rolling away. I
pursue the pest, batting it and swatting it and
chasing it out of the sleeping quarters and down
the corridor. *You can't escape the Queen! No
one can!* I bound about as it continues to scurry
away. I take one large, lobbed, leap and end up

head-butting it and me into the floor. I shake off the stars that I see and funnel the tiny beast under my body and sit on it. Queen Shorty, the Vanquisher! I fall to the side, holding the creature in my claws as my hind legs beat it into submission. I check my quest. Success! It moves not! What's this? Movement. Out the corner of my eye. The Simpleton! It's upon me, wanting to plunder my prey. *Have at it, Simpleton, I've already bested the pest.*

I run down the corridor, slip between a servant's stumps, veer through the towers, jump to my couch, and then vault to the top of a barricade currently being erected or dismantled by a servant. *What hast thou planned for these battlements. Speak, slave!* My eyes wild, my Beautiful Tail in charge. "What the frrrllll?" I trill reflexively as the servant's gaudy hands take hold of my delicate frame and violently toss me across the room. (Well, they put me down gently, but their intent was more than apparent!)

I lick the sordid scent of old sneakers off my fine coat and glare at the human who I believe is carrying old sneaker out of the green stone. What insolence! The other servant is walking to the cooking gallery so I hurry and walk in front of them to voice my distaste for disloyalty. What's this? The servant stomps right past, swiping at my Beautiful Tail! It's all right, my Beautiful Tail. I wash my Beautiful Tail of the dirty scents left behind. I lick and clean and wash and preen. Aye, 'tis good to feel clean. 'Tis good to feel this floor of wooden planks. I roll onto my back and stretch my legs long, extending my claws and relish in the reach. A servant comes upon me and I curl my front paws in and gaze up at them with my belly exposed. When they are stressed and reeking of cinnamon, this tactic always freshens the air and has them emitting a pleasant smell of peaches and plums as they address me softly in a lilting brogue.

"Oh, my Queen, thou art the cutest and sweetest and most precious of all the earth's creatures." I turn my head up and curve my body like the letter C. *I know.* I let their now fragrant fingers tousle the fur under my chin and behind my ears. I wonder if they will try for the belly? Their hand pulls away and brushes against my front paws. Yes, yes, I think they will. Their hand ventures lower to my white undercoat. *Tee hee!* The first one tickles. Oh, joy! The second one prickles. I stare at them, wide-eyed, Beautiful Tail a flurry. *Come on, servant, I dare you.* And a third! Yes! I take hold of their hand with all paws and careful claws, grabbing their fingers to chomp down ever so lightly. Dutiful wards they are, I must remind them who's in charge, you see. I grant leniency upon their protestation and release them. I roll onto my front and sit up to take stock of my surroundings.

Night has fallen. The servants are closing the lights one by one. The Simpleton watches my every move from atop a tower of green stones. My couch is in place, my chair is prepared for me, my rug is ready for my expressions of displeasure. My new castle seems quieter than the last, less echoes traveling down the corridor, less shiny elephants rumbling by outside. I inhale deeply which turns into a massive yawn. All lights are out now and the servants have retired to their sleeping quarters. I venture down the castle corridor for a last inspection and to attend to some last-minute doodie duty.

Ah, my poopsies depository. I am grateful it survived the battle, though I admit I would not have been opposed to soiling this entire castle if 'twere not up to snuff. I would have also enjoyed seeing the servants argue about the reason, wondering what "message" I was sending. Thus far, the dwelling is proving sufficient but I shall be keeping notes to possibly send "messages" at a later date. The humans think we don't know what we're doing if we "miss" the litter box, but trust me, we know exactly what we're doing.

But on with the business at hand, and then a follow-up scratch upon the plastic dome. *scratch-scritch-scrape-scratch.* The business, unfortunately, is not being buried as my instincts suggest it should. Indeed, my only quarrel with the plastic dome is that it does a poor job in covering my poopsies. *scrape-scratch-scritch-scratch.* Hm. *sniff-sniff.* There is no change. *scrape-scrap-scritch-scratch.* Hm. *sniff-sniff.* Or perhaps there is. My instincts whisper to me that this scratching motion will remove my waste from my sight, but scratching the plastic dome does little more than amuse me which is honestly good enough for me. 'Tis a pleasing sound, my nails on this scratchy surface. Oh, joyous sounds, quite musical really! The repetition is calming, familiar, like I've done this before but I can't say that I recall. I go faster and faster. *scrape-scratch-scrap-scritch-scrape-scrap-*

"QUEEN!" a servant bellows from the sleeping quarters. "WHAT BEAUTIFUL MUSIC THOU HAST BESTOWED UPON US! THANK YOU, YOUR HIGHNESS!" Ah, my doting servants are always appreciative of my talents, and it is good.

I make my way through the castle once more, avoiding and cursing the mess the servants have made. Green stones, half-empty boxes, barricades and towers misplaced. If I weren't exhausted from missing my catnaps today I might take it upon myself to do some more investigating and rearranging. But alas, my head, heavy from the crown, needs to rest. I spy the Simpleton nestled beneath the couch, half-sleeping and keeping a lazy eye trained on my every move. I venture into the sleeping quarters and tuck just inside the bed frame beneath the cover of night. *O'er the hem and 'neath the bed, I slink to rest my weary head...*

Chapter 7

Movement. A sliver of light. Clanging from the eating gallery. *"Fooood!"* A *crack*, a *creeeaaak*, a *slurp*, and the *clinking* of metal on glass.

Yaaawwwnnn.

Streeetch.

Sleeeeep.

Chapter 8

I do not want to move. My body is heavy, glued to the floor. I can barely lift my head. But my tummy is telling me I must, certain that a feast has been prepared for me. Or perhaps it was a dream. I open my eyes and manage to stand up as best as I can beneath the bed frame. I reach my front legs out and drop my chest to the floor, then extend my chest forward as I stretch out my hind legs, first the right then the left. I sit on my haunches and debate the pros and cons of going back to sleep. I can sleep or I can eat. An hour passes and I decide I prefer the latter, so I lift myself through the space between the headboard and the bed and slowly remind my legs how to function as I stagger to the eating gallery. The floor feels softer than the usual cursed concrete and I am reminded that the servants have appointed my new quarters with actual flooring finally, as if that's something that even needs consideration. Dimwits.

The sun shines brightly into my new castle, cutting through the jungle of boxes and barricades, casting shadows on the wall. I look hard at the phantoms for I will have to attack and banish them as they are a vile threat to our security. Though their wits may be dim, my wards remain satisfactory providers, and it is up to the leader to protect the weak. But after breakfast.

As I suspected, the servants woke early and hunted for the day's provisions, though my bowl is oddly half-empty. I glare at the Simpleton licking its chops from outside the water chamber, surely waiting for its master to ask it who is a "good boy." *They don't mean you, you brainless beast!* If Picasso painted an impression of a panda, where nothing goes where it should on a beast of black and white, you might get an idea of what the Simpleton looks like. I quickly lap up what remains of the hunt.

The servant exits the water chamber down the corridor and ignores the Simpleton's wails. They approach me as I walk toward them, my head and Beautiful Tail high.

Good morrow, dutiful ward. I say, it is a splendid day, isn't it? My Beautiful Tail punctuates my greeting with a question mark.

"'Tis, my Queen. I hope you enjoy your new home. We secured it just for you." I rub my cheek on their leg followed by the rest of my body and every inch of my Beautiful Tail. The servant smells of peaches and plums and me, and all is well.

I follow them as they head to the front room. I leap onto my couch and begin to bathe myself with my tongue and the rays of the sun and watch as the servant removes items from green stones to place about the castle. I squint into the sunlight and beyond. I can see from my tower several stories high the shiny elephants rumbling past, the townspeople meandering along, fluffy-tailed vermin skittering across ropes and wires, the odd flying rat swooping sarcastically by. We shan't do battle today, my peasants. I declare it a day of peace and rest. But that market across the way with the blue-hued awning where the commoners are queueing could mean trouble in the future. That warrants further investigation. There is also an occasional and faint howling just beyond my castle's drawbridge in the hall. What or who could that be? What manner of beasts lie in the realm of this new world? And there is one locked door at the end of the hall that I have yet to access. What mystery are the servants hiding from me? Yes, there is much work to do in expanding my benevolent rule here in my new Queendom, but that is for another day.

...

I am stirred awake by a shuffle. A kerfuffle? An upheaval! Oh, no, 'tis just the servant hammering at the wall. Perhaps they are killing a sprite! I slant my ears back but stay wide-eyed. *I say, that is admirable work, ward, but do keep it down.* Dimwits.

I yawn and readjust my head and stretch out my feetsies. What's this? A warmth beside me. 'Tis the Simpleton, stealing my own body's heat! It looks up at me with tired, weary eyes, its ears slanted sideways ready for my deft left upon its unoccupied noggin. But none will come today. Before putting my head down to sleep again, I narrow my eyes and flit my right ear back. *Sniff my butt and you're dead.*

About the author

Rob lives in Toronto with his partner, Bryan (pictured), and their two cats, Shorty and Kodi. He is a fitness trainer, photographer, and writer. He loves traveling (which his cats don't like), writing at home (which his cats do like), and playing piano (they're divided on that one). He won the 2014 Golden Kitty People's Choice Award for best cat video at the Internet Cat Film Festival in Minneapolis. Yes, there is such a thing. Both Shorty and Kodi were adopted from Toronto shelters. If you are considering becoming a guardian to an animal companion, please visit your local shelter as there is a homeless cat or dog waiting just for you.

Made in the USA
Middletown, DE
06 June 2021